APR   2023

A **MIDDLE SCHOOL** STORY

DOG DIARIES

BIG TOP BONANZA

A **MIDDLE SCHOOL** STORY

DOG DIARIES

BIG TOP BONANZA

JAMES PATTERSON

WITH STEVEN BUTLER

ILLUSTRATED BY RICHARD WATSON

JIMMY Patterson Books
Little, Brown and Company
New York   Boston

Copyright © 2021 by James Patterson
Illustrations by Richard Watson
Cover art by Ellie O'Shea. Cover design by Tracy Shaw.
Cover copyright © 2023 by Hachette Book Group, Inc.

JIMMY Patterson Books / Little, Brown and Company

Hachette Book Group
1290 Avenue of the Americas, New York, NY 10104
Kids.JamesPatterson.com

Originally published in Great Britain in 2021
by Penguin Random House UK

First U.S. Edition: April 2023

JIMMY Patterson Books is an imprint of Little, Brown and Company, a division of Hachette Book Group, Inc. The Little, Brown name and logo are trademarks of Hachette Book Group, Inc. The JIMMY Patterson Books® name and logo are trademarks of JBP Business, LLC.

The publisher is not responsible for websites (or their content) that are not owned by the publisher.

Library of Congress Cataloging-in-Publication Data

Names: Patterson, James, 1947– author. | Butler, Steven, 1983– author. | Watson, Richard, 1980– illustrator.
Title: Big top bonanza / by James Patterson with Steven Butler ; illustrated by Richard Watson.
Description: First U.S. edition. | New York : JIMMY Patterson Books/ Little, Brown and Company, 2023. | Series: Dog diaries | Originally published in Great Britain in 2021 by Penguin Random House UK. | Audience: Ages 7–12. | Summary: "Junior is in for a BARKing big adventure when the circus comes to town!" —Provided by publisher.
Identifiers: LCCN 2022031469 | ISBN 9780316411028 | ISBN 9780316411127 (ebook)
Subjects: CYAC: Dogs--Fiction. | Circus—Fiction. | Diaries—Fiction. | Humorous stories. | LCGFT: Humorous fiction. | Novels.
Classification: LCC PZ7.P27653 Bi 2022 | DDC [Fic]—dc23
LC record available at https://lccn.loc.gov/2022031469

ISBNs: 978-0-316-41102-8 (paper over board), 978-0-316-41112-7 (ebook)

Printed in the United States of America

LSC-C

Printing 1, 2023

For Steven Lenton and Big-Eared Bob.
My family pack.
—S.B.

Roll up! Roll up, one and all! Follow the band and feast your person-peepers on the GRRReatest show in town!

Welcome to P.T. BARK-HAM'S waggy-tail-tastic circus!

You won't believe the lick-a-lumptious things you'll see. Grab yourself a bucket of popping-cornies...whatever that is...and come take a seat for the show of a lifetime!

Watch the muscly-
mastiffs lifting the
mightiest of weights!

Marvel at the tumbling toy poodles and the clowning corgis!

Gawp at the fearless French bulldogs on the flying trapeze!

Then maybe take a walk around the carnival? You could try your luck on the ring toss or take a trip to see Madame Nose-A-Lot in her spooky tent. Her sniff-a-licious snout can snuffle-out your fortune in a jiffy.

If you're feeling brave, take a deep breath and meet Mr. Reek. His pungent perfume is revolting to humans but all kinds of whiff-tastic to any woofy-watchers in the audience!

Yep! P.T. BARK-HAM'S circus is the best-best-BESTEST thing you'll ever see. It's better than tummy rubs!

OH, WHO AM I KIDDING? Nothing is better than tummy rubs! Ha ha!

Now, I bet you NEVER would have guessed... 'cause I'm a master of doggy disguise... but I'm not really P.T. BARK-HAM! I was just yankin' ya tail!

Have you guessed who I really am?

It's me!

Junior! How are you, my person-pal? I can't even begin to describe how good it feels to smell your human scent and know you're holding my latest MUTT MANUAL in your five-fingery-digits.

So much has happened since you last read one of my books and...WAIT! What am I thinking? I'm getting way too excited and not concentrating. I can't help it...I'm SO barky-brained sometimes.

Maybe you haven't read any of my AMAZ-ING Dog Diaries before...if this is the first time our pawy-paths have crossed, we need a proper introduction, right?

HELLO! It's great to meet you. You seem like the perfect person-type to be reading my newest adventure and OH, BOY is it a doozy!

Just in case you're new to all this, my name is Junior Catch-A-Doggy-Bone and I live in a town called Hills Village with my very own person-pack. Ever since they rescued me from Pooch Prison and brought me into their great big kennel, it's been Fun with a capital F!

I'll introduce you...

There's Mom-Lady...

~~Mrs Khatchadorian~~

Mom-Lady
Catch-A-Doggy-
Bone

She's in charge of the Food Room and buys the treats. I love having her around.

Then there's Jawjaw…

~~Georgia Khatchadorian~~

Jawjaw

Catch-A-Doggy-Bone

Watch out for this pawty pooper. She's a little snappy at times and likes to call me a ba...a bad...a bad do...do...dog! I can barely bring myself to say it! UGH!

Grandmoo's a howly hoot!

~~Grandma~~

Grandmoo

13

She gives me the scratchiest scratches behind my ears.

Then there's…AH…I saved the best for last, my person-pal! My tail has already gone into waggy overdrive at the thought of saying his name.

The BESTEST pet human a dog like me could wish for…

RUFF!

~~Rafe Khatchadorian~~

Ruff
Catch-A-
Doggy-Bone

Have you ever heard a lovelier, more mutt-tastic name in your whole licky-life? ME NEITHER!

We've had the most TERRIFIC adventures together...sometimes howl-arious...sometimes jaw-janglingly scary...but Ruff has always been there to share a treat or two and curl up with at the end of every action-packed day. SIGH!

Anyway, what was I saying? I got a little distracted there for a moment. If I do any more daydreaming about my paw-fect pet human, I'll be happy-dancing all week...then I'll never get to tell you my story.

Now, I know what's going on in that non-barky-brain of yours. You're scratching your human head right now, wondering why I was pretending to be P.T. BARK-HAM: RINGMASTER EXTRAORDINAIRE.

I'll explain everything, my furless friend, I promise.

Are you sitting comfortably? Good!

Do you have extra snacks to keep your taste buds tingling while you read? You do? Good!

It all started yesterday...

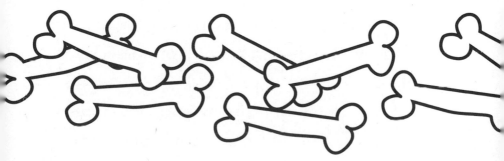

Tuesday

8:57 a.m.

It was just another morning here in Hills Village, my person-pal. As normal as any other. Ruff and Jawjaw had stuffed their backpacks with ink-sticks, booky-things, and snacks for lunch, and headed off for a day at school.

Now, don't get me wrong, my furless friend. I hate it SO much when Ruff heads out and jumps on the big yellow moving people-box on wheels every day at 7:30 a.m. sharp.

I swear, it's awful, my person-pal. THE WORST! It breaks my houndy heart when Ruff goes away, and I have a strict list of EXTREMELY IMPORTANT chores I SIMPLY HAVE to perform every time he leaves or I just couldn't call myself a GOOD BOY.

Ruff Leaving To-Do List

* Howl at the window – 20 mins
* Whine at the front door – 10 mins
* Panic-poop in Jawjaw's bedroom – 5 mins
* Go back to the window for more howling
                                    – 15 mins
* Sulk under Ruff's bed or in the
        laundry pile – 7 mins
* Eat a few Crunchy-Lumps or
  Doggo-Drops   to make myself
      feel better – 3 mins

By 8:30 a.m. I'm normally all done with my yappy-chores and back to my happy, houndy self, ready for a morning walk with Mom-Lady and some playtime with my best pooch-pals in the nearby dog park.

Yesterday, just like normal, Mom-Lady was holding on to the end of my leash and I was leading her where I wanted to go. We'd taken the long route around town, past Belly Burstin' Burgers and the Dandy-Dog store, so she could fetch a few things from the the grocery store. I didn't mind, of course. Being a masterful mutt, I worked out ages ago that if I sit quietly outside the store in my best GOOD BOY pose while Mom-Lady shops, she brings me a cube of cheese or slice of meat from the delicious-smelling BELLY-catessen counter.

Doesn't it sound awesome? I swear, my paws get tingly at the thought of it. I've never seen the BELLY-catessen counter myself, but I imagine it's a wonder to behold. A houndy haven. A pooch paradise. SNACK-TROPOLIS!

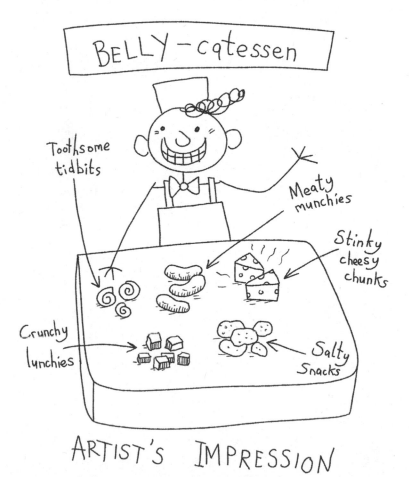

ARTIST'S IMPRESSION

So, I was still chewing on the last scraps of the latest greasy chicken-y GOOD BOY treat Mom-Lady bought me as we wandered away from the grocery store. We were turning the street corner near the dog park gates when...

I couldn't believe it, my furless friend! I'd never, in all my life, seen the dog park closed. And that's not all…

There were big, boomy hammering sounds and lots of yelling and yowling coming from beyond the gate. I couldn't see what was making all the racket because of the great big sign on the gate that definitely hadn't been there the day before. I know, because I would have peed on it if it had. Ha ha!

Normally, my understanding of the Peoplish language is terrific…well…very good… well…it's okay…all right, I admit, it's crumby at the best of times, but I can read a word or two. Only, the letters on this sign were all twisty and loopy, and I couldn't figure any of it out.

Luckily for me, it was that time of the morning when, just like canine-clockwork, all the local pooches of Hills Village bring their pet humans for a stroll across the playing field or a chase around the jungle gym. Before I knew it, my very own pack-pals had arrived.

Would you just look at 'em!

We've been through a whole heap of chaos and adventure-tastic trouble together, let me tell you, my furless friend. We all met back in our days at Hills Village Dog Shelter—POOCH PRISON!—and since then we've learned that nothing, and I mean NOTHING, is too weird to happen in our town.

So, what was this peculiar sign all about?

Everyone was as SHOCKED as I was when they saw it, my person-pal.

All the humans stood around in groups, chattering in their Peoplish language about the catastrophic closure. While they were distracted, my mutt-mates and I did a little investigating...they don't call us the INTERNATIONAL SNOOP SQUAD for nothing, you know? Umm...okay...no one calls us that, but they would if they knew how

FANTASTIC we all are at solving mysteries and snuffling for clues.

Betty was the last to show up that morning. We all sat around, trying our hardest to be patient, which is NOT easy for a pack of curious canines, but as soon as Betty arrived, we quickly brought her over to the sign.

You see, Betty's pet human is one of those teachy-types who works at the local elementary school. I've met this kind of human before and they can sometimes be a little grumpy and serious...like Ruff's TERRIFYING teachy-type, Principal Stricker...but Betty's pet human is nothing like that. She's fun and kind, and always curls up with Betty on the comfy squishy thing at night to read what the human-pups in her class have written in their booky-things.

Anyway...because of all the ready-writey-snuggles, Betty has picked up more than her fair share of understanding when it comes to reading you peoples' weird way of writing.

Humans, always overcomplicating things! When us dogs want to leave a message for others, we just pee or poop on whatever it is we're talking about and the job is done. After a few snuffly sniffs, the message is received, and everything is totally clear to us mutts. But humans? Don't get me started on how confusing all your dots and swirls and dashes are…

So…there we were, outside the dog park gates, and Betty was doing her best to decipher this mysterious sign.

MR. BINGO! In no time, my mutt-mind started to race with questions. Who was Mr. Bingo? Why was he here? What in the world did he think he was doing, closing the dog park?

I tell ya, my person-pal. My barky-blood was about to boil with furry frustration. We were all here, ready and raring to go for our happy walkies, howling and splashing around the duck pond, and we weren't able to because…

Mr Bingo's Traveling Carnival and Circus!

Wait...was that...A CARNIVAL?! A CIR-CUS?! My houndy-heart was beating so fast I thought I might explode into a squillion pooch pieces. My pooch-pack all started to bark and bound about in excitement. Who could have known when we woke up that morning that something so WAG-NIFICENT would happen? I told you, there's never a quiet moment in Hills Village...

Now, you're probably wondering how on earth a bunch of mutts like us know about circus things, right? Well, the answer is simple...

Way back when we were prisoner-pups in Hills Village Dog Shelter, long before we all moved in with our person-packs, there was a raggedy chow chow in the cage next to ours who LOVED to tell stories.

Mama Mange was her name, and if you've read any of my Dog Diaries before you'll know all about that flea-bitten old rascal.

Late at night, when Pooch Prison was dark and scary, and the promise of treats and tummy rubs seemed far, far away, Mama Mange would delight everyone with tales of her amazing adventures around the world.

One thing's for sure, that worn-out woofer knew how to LIVE!

One time I barked so loud it cracked the Liberty Bell...

> Yellowstone National Park was renamed YOWLY-BONE GNASH-EM-ALL PARK after I buried all my best snacks there one summer!

I tell ya, my person-pal...I don't know how we would have survived that horrible place without Mama Mange's stories to brighten the mood.

Some of my absolute favorite tail-wagging

tales were from her life in the circus…

Back when she was a puppy, in the days when everything was black and white, Mama's paw-paw was a super-famous dare-devil called…

HORATIO THE WONDER DOG!

He can leap through a ring of fire!
He can walk on a wire!
He can juggle 100 balls at once!

Mama Mange toured from country to country with her daring dog-dad for years, astounding audiences, wowing the world, and meeting the crowned heads of Europe.

I've never forgotten those stories. I can't believe an actual really-real circus is coming to Hills Village Dog Park! My tail is going crazy just thinking about it!

The only thing that could make this day EVEN better was if Mama Mange was still around to see the fun...I wish she was. She'd love an evening of excitement and reminiscing about her days in the circus, I just know it!

If you've been reading my Dog Diaries, you might remember that my mutt-mates and I helped the scampery-scamp escape the clutches of POOCH PRISON in a runaway hot tub when we were on vacation at the Rambling Ridge Campground...

The last I heard of Mama Mange, she was living the high life in Hollywood! According to her, they now call it HOWLY-WOOD in her honor. BRILLIANT!

She really is a one-of-a-kind canine, and thanks to her, I know all about what to expect when Mr. Bingo's Traveling Carnival and Circus opens.

I can't wait!

You can imagine how torturous it was for the whole of yesterday and last night. After Mom-Lady yanked me back home, it was all I could think about! I spent the whole afternoon imagining what wonders I was going to see and smell and taste, and last night when Ruff let me out into the backyard for my pre-sleepy-time pee, I managed to jump onto the trash cans for a peek over the fence…

All over the town I could see dogs leaning out of windows, clambering onto garden shed roofs and lumber piles for a glimpse into the dog park to see what was happening…and it all looked AMAZING!

Wednesday

6:30 a.m.

So, there you have it, my person-pal. You've caught up with the story so far, and I'm sure you can understand why I was pretending to be P.T. BARK-HAM. The circus is all I can think about!

Last night in bed, while Ruff was gently snoozing, I lay there for hours as visions of cartwheeling cavapoos swirled through my mind. I'm surprised I got any sleep at all!

But…today is finally here. I'm wide awake and itching to go to the circus this evening. I just have to keep calm and try not to explode with eagerness and impatience before Ruff gets back from school, then we can all venture off for the most BARKTASTIC night of our lives!

AAAAGH! This is going to be tricky. I'm already waiting for Ruff to arrive home and he hasn't even gone to school yet.

Only an hour until he's off on the big yellow moving people-box on wheels…

The sooner Ruff goes, the sooner he'll return…

It's only an hour…that's all…easy…you can do this, Junior!

Just sixty minutes…

SIXTY WHOLE MINUTES?!?!? AGH! This is going to be tough!!!

7:43 a.m.

Okay, my furless friend. Ruff has FINALLY gone to school, which means that we're a teensy bit closer to visiting Mr. Bingo's carnival.

Never in my wildest dreams did I imagine a time when I'd look forward to Ruff leaving in the morning, but this is an extra-special case. I couldn't even focus on my usual Ruff-leaving yappy-chores...I tried, but my houndy-heart just wasn't in it...

10:48 a.m.

Is it possible to sprain your tail, my person-pal?

48

With all the excitement and nervousness, I've been wagging my tail so much I think it might fall off!

Earlier, I took Mom-Lady out for our morning stroll and dragged her straight to the dog park for a nose around. She wanted to wander over to the post office, but there are times when a pet human needs to listen to its doggy-master, and today was definitely one of those times.

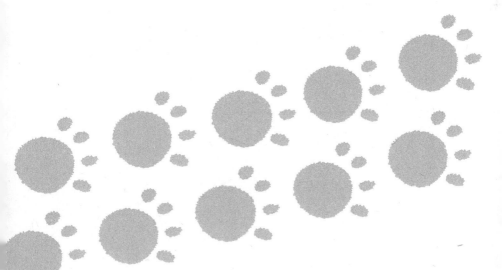

When we arrived at the park gates, I saw the big sign was still in place and there were lots of other dogs and their humans snuffling about. They seemed to be gathered around something that I couldn't see from the street corner, and there was no way I was going to miss whatever it was they were ogling. Junior Catch-A-Doggy-Bone does not wait at the back of crowds and miss out on all the fun, I'll have you know!

So, with Mom-Lady in tow, I dived snout-first through the group of people and pooches. My nose was twitching and my jowls were jabbering with excitement. What could it be? Maybe it was Mr. Bingo him-self...?!

AAAAAGGGGGHHHHHH!!!!!

I was so determined to get to the front of the gathering, my paws were ten paces ahead of my barky-brain. Just as I pushed my way between a slobbery Saint Bernard and his fidgety pet lady, I looked up and... I...I don't know if I even have the words to describe it...I...I looked up and...and... saw the most HORRIFIC...the most hackle-raising...the most monstrous man-thing I've ever clapped my eyes on in my licky-life! It made all the beasties that ran around town on the night of the HOWLY WIENER look like cute little kittens!

I've never seen anything like it before, my person-pal! The carnival monster seemed to be smiling, but everything about it was bizarre and wrong. There was strange white stuff all over its face and its hair was the same color as Ruff's favorite pair of under-pants! The thing's clothes were loose and patched together, and the bright-red shoes were big enough to fit ten human-paws into each one! It was holding great big floaty blobs-on-strings in its hand, and they smelled like morning breath and toothpaste.

What was this thing?!?! I was just about to run away as fast as I could, when the man-monster-thing thrust a flyer into Mom-Lady's hand...and then...then it laughed, waved, and vanished through the gate behind the big sign...

What was even more shocking is that none of the humans seemed even the tiniest bit scared of the man-monster. Mom-Lady even let out a little unexpected chuckle. I'll never understand you humans...

When we got back to the Catch-A-Doggy-Bone kennel, Mom-Lady put the flyer down on the Food Room table. As soon as I got the chance, I hopped up onto one of the chairs to have a good look...

The fur on my back stood on end, my person-pal. The man-monster had given Mom-Lady a map of the carnival and it looks...it looks completely WONDERFUL! More than wonderful...WAG-NIFICENT!

I can't wait to go on all the rides! With names like that, they've got to be good! The Furry Wheel sounds like the paw-fect amusement for a dog and his mutt-mates to enjoy…and at the center of it all…the BIG TOP! It looks like a giant flappy kennel. I bet all the funniest, noisiest, oohiest and ahhiest action takes place in there.

I'm certain this is going to be a day…and night…to remember! I just have to while away the rest of the day. It's going to be tricky…

Wish me luck!

11:17 a.m.

Okay...this isn't so bad. All I have to do is relax in the sunshine patch on the Picture Box Room carpet and not think about the circus. AGH! I just said CIRCUS! NOW I'M THINKING ABOUT IT AGAIN!!!

11:22 a.m.

Just breathe, Junior!
    Breathe in...
    Breathe out...
    Breathe in...
    Breathe out...

11:30 a.m.

It's time for my mid-morning nap. That'll help me pass the time. If I can get to sleep, that is. I'm so excited I don't think I could even—zzz zzzzzzzzzzzzzzzzzzzzzzzzzzzzzzzzzzz...

12:16 p.m.

Ugh! That didn't work, my person-pal! As soon as I drifted off I was dreaming about being P.T. BARK-HAM again! I think I suit a mustache! Quite the dashing dog if you ask me...

12:39 p.m.

I've been staring at the time-circle on the Food Room wall, but it's moving so slowly it would make even the most tranquil of terriers tear about the place in torturous torment.

Think, Junior...there are loads of things you can do to pass the time...

62

WHAT AM I THINKING? I'm a dog! I can't do any of those things!

It's about time I do something I'm actually good at...hmmmmm...oh, I know...I'll poop in Jawjaw's shoes. She loves it when I do that, and I am very good at it.

PROBLEM SOLVED!!!

5:28 p.m.

I don't know how I managed it, my person-pal, but I somehow got through the day.

Believe me when I tell you there wasn't a shoe I didn't poop in, not a bird or raccoon I didn't bark at in the backyard, not a single corner of the kennel I didn't sniff. BUT I DID IT!

Ruff and Jawjaw are home from school and they're already in their rooms getting changed before we head out. Jawjaw did a lot of screaming at first…I think she was just really happy about finding all the poops in her shoes…but they're all finally nearly ready for the noisiest, rumbliest, laughiest, best-best-BESTEST night of our lives. I just know it's going to be great!

6:06 p.m.

This is it, my furless friend. Ruff, Jawjaw, and Mom-Lady all bundled out into the evening air, with me leading the way. Grandmoo even joined us, and we're all heading to the dog park and the wonders of Mr. Bingo's Traveling Carnival.

I can already hear the music, and there

are all sorts of new smells in the air. This is going to be waggy-tail-icious!

6:14 p.m.

BE STILL, MY HOUNDY-HEART! We've just arrived at the dog park gates and there are dogs and people EVERYWHERE! You should see it, my person-pal! The big sign has been removed and the gates are wide open, revealing thousands of flashy lights and swoopy rides and sizzly food stalls just waiting to be explored. I think I've died and gone to houndy heaven!

AAAGH! And my pooch-pack are all here with their pet humans, too. Lola's owner has even dressed her up for the occasion. What is it with you humans making us pooches wear costumes??? Ha ha! She looks…she looks…

66

6:17 p.m.

AAAAAND WE'RE IN! There's so much to see…SO MUCH TO DO! I…I…don't think my barky-brain can…can cope…with…with…so…much…so much…dog-tastic…I…might explode! I might howl forever! I might…I…I can feel it coming…happy dance commencing in five…four…three…two…

6:20 p.m.

Well, that was a little embarrassing, my fur-less friend. The overload of AMAZING things to sniff and bark and look at had me happy-dancing like a puppy at playtime...

Now who looks silly? Ha ha!

69

Anyway…now I've got my happy dance out of the way and Lola got a chance to make fun of me in return…I guess I deserved it…I'm off for a snoop and a sniff.

You should see this place, my furless friend. It's incredible!

Mom-Lady, Jawjaw, and Grandmoo have gone off to look at the boring rides in the far corner of the park. Ha! Can you believe they want to go on the Sleepy Slides and the Lullabicycles when there are proper, whoop-de-doo-tious rides to have fun on?

No INTERNATIONAL MUTT OF MYSTERY would be caught dead on the Lazy Lily Pads or the Calming Cuddle Cars, but OH BOY are there some scary-looking attractions that are just perfect for an adventurous pooch like me.

70

But which one first? I think the Vomit Comet is a good place to start. Now, I'll just lead Ruff in that direction and…

WHAT?!?! I...I...I CAN'T BELIEVE IT, MY PERSON-PAL! Why in the world would dogs not be allowed on the spine-jabbering roller coasters? I've waited all day for this and... and...IT'S NOT FAIR! This always happens to me, my furless friend. If it's not rides I can't go on, its museums that won't let me snack on their dino-roar bones, or doggy health spas that only serve vegetables, or camping vacations where I'm stuck in the tent next to IONA STRICKER, the most evil human in all of Hills Village! My life is one big ball of NO!!!!

NO!!!!

6:33 p.m.

Okay, I've calmed down a bit now, my person-pal. I'm sorry about making a scene back there. I'm just so emotional this evening. I think I might be a little hungry or overtired... yeah...that's it. If you've read any of my diaries before, you'll know I'm NEVER dramatic...except for that one time...oh, and the other time...and another time when I heard that thing about the thing...but apart from that I'm ALMOST NEVER dramatic.

So...just when I thought I was going to sink into a never-ending pit of doggy-despair where I was destined to wallow in my own misery for ever and ever, Ruff suggested we go check out the food stalls and...well...what kind of mutt would I be to turn down such an offer? Ha ha!

7:05 p.m.

Yowzers! I swear to you, my furless friend, I could visit Mr. Bingo's carnival every night this week and I wouldn't get a chance to try all the amazing food they've got here. Everything smells so LICK-A-LUMPTIOUS! There's a kind of sizzly, spicy, smoky scent in the air and it's making my super sniff-a-licious snout twitch with glee.

Ruff tried a few snacks from THE GREASE TRAP: DEEP-FRIED EVERYTHING.

I snaffled a couple of tasty tidbits from BURNING BEAGLE: SIZZLE DOGS.

Don't panic…they're not actually made from…oh, you know!

Then Ruff stuffed himself with delicious-smelling stringy things from OODLES OF NOODLES

OODLES OF NOODLES

while I had a cheesy and hammy-licious sandy-wish (I think that's how you humans say it) from ANOTHER ONE BITES THE CRUST.

ANOTHER ONE BITES THE CRUST

This place is a foodish fantasy land. Who needs to ride the Vomit Comet or the Child Churner when there's so much food-fun to be had?

Next I think I wanna try DON'T GO BACON MY HEART.

Or maybe PENNE FOR YOUR THOUGHTS.

7:15 p.m.

AGH! This is the moment we've all been waiting for, my person-pal! Ruff and I were happily digging into a bowl of pasta when a trumpet sounded across the whole carnival, and everyone fell silent…a bright light shone on the entrance to the big flappy kennel at the center of all the chaos, and a man with a big tall hat stepped outside.

It was…it was…MR. BINGO!!!

Dazzled? DAZZLED? I've been scared and surprised and delighted and hungry and howly and poopy and nervous and snoozy and sniffy and gloomy and happy and houndy...BUT I'VE NEVER BEEN DAZZLED BEFORE! I can't even begin to imagine what circus-ish wonders we're about to witness. I hope it will be every bit as magical as the stories Mama Mange told us...here goes, my furless friend...we're heading in...

7:20 p.m.

I...I...I don't understand, my person-pal... everything has gone wrong again! What did us mutts do to deserve this? I can't think straight...my mouth has gone dry...my tail is tucked under...we...we...we're NOT ALLOWED TO WATCH THE CIRCUS?!?!?!

All right, calm down, Junior. Give me a second, my furless friend…and another second…just one more…

Okay, I'm back in calmsville again. I'll tell you what happened…so, there we were, heading toward the entrance to the big flappy kennel, when another of those big brutish carnival workers stopped Ruff and…

No dogs allowed inside the Big Top.

Why does Mr. Bingo hate us dogs SO much? And to make matters worse...just when I thought Ruff would stand up to the grumpy guy and fight for me, demanding to take me inside, he and the rest of my pooch-pack's pet humans all turned to us and said...

You wait here, boy. I'll be back soon.

What?

Well, this is just great!

Tonight was supposed to be the most exciting night of my life, but I can't ride the Vomit Comet or the Child Churner or the Haunted Howler and NOW we're not allowed to watch the circus, EITHER?!

I can hear the band getting ready to play inside the big flappy kennel, and I feel more miserable than an empty food bowl. I'm just going to curl up here and cry myself to sleep...

7:26 p.m.

Check! Check! This is Secret Agent Catch-A-Doggy-Bone reporting for duty. Don't despair, my person-pal. If there's one thing my MUTT-MANUALS will teach you, it's that you can always find fun, even when things look downright dismal.

I was just about to flop face-first into the grass and have a good moan to myself, when Genghis, that tricksy little hero, came up with a BRILLIANT idea.

Psst! Under here, you guys. We can sneak in...

We didn't wait even for a second, my fur-less friend. When you're an INTERNATIONAL MUTT OF MYSTERY you've got to act quickly and make super-fast decisions without even thinking. It's the smartest way, I swear.

Anyway, before anyone said another word, we all scrambled under the flappy ken-nel walls and found ourselves in a sort of...I don't know what...for a second, I thought it was a cage, until I realized that all the hori-zontal wooden bars were actually rows of plank-ish seats. We could see hundreds of human feet dangling in the gaps!

I spotted Ruff's shoes straight away. Well, they're super easy to sniff out. No one else's pet human in all of Hills Village has sneakers that smell so sweetly of stinky socks, mud, and mischief. DELISH!

Being very careful, I sneaked over and found I could see the circus ring perfectly between Ruff's feet and…now, I don't want to sound too slobbery and sentimental, but it felt nice knowing I was going to watch the show so close to my AMAZING pet human… even if he did leave me outside. Hmmm… I'll give him a little telling-off tomorrow and deny him a face lick or two when he gets home from school.

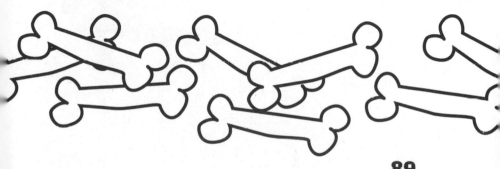

7:30 p.m.

It's time, my person-pal! All the lights went out and Mr. Bingo has appeared in the center of the ring. My tail is going into waggy overdrive! This is going to be BRILLIANT!

7:56 p.m.

AGH! That was the most STUPENDOUS thing my pooch-peepers have ever seen, my furless friend! We watched swingy high-flying humans whizzing about in the air...

And the terrifying man-monsters were back…but all the humans loved them and couldn't stop laughing!

There was a lady juggling a squillion balls at once. I don't know what it is about a bouncy ball, but it just makes us dog-types go bonkers. I had to grip my paws to the floor to stop myself from running out onto the stage and chasing her around in circles.

Everything was so AMAZING I couldn't help howling and yowling with joy, but luckily the music was loud enough that nobody could hear me. Not even Ruff…

8:35 p.m.

STOP EVERYTHING!!!! I THINK I MUST BE SEEING THINGS THAT AREN'T THERE!

It can't be true, my person-pal! It just can't be! I don't even know how to start describing to you what I've just seen in the circus ring.

I…I…was sitting there in the dark between Ruff's feet. Happily watching the show, when Mr. Bingo walked out…

And now for our star act!
Fresh from the palaces of Paris,
the grand courts of Copenhagen, the
music halls of Havana. I present:
MADEMOISELLE MANGE!

Before she even appeared, I caught a whiff of something familiar in the air. It was a kind of dusty, rusty, sour smell, and I knew it was her. I'd recognize her scent anywhere!

My mind started to race, but before I could even begin to understand it all, a horse galloped out into the ring, and sitting on its back, wearing a headdress of pink feathers and sparkly sequins, was…was…

~~Mademoiselle~~ Mange
MAMA

98

I didn't know whether to laugh, poop, or cry as that wily old chow chow came trotting into view and started performing the most incredible act I'd ever seen. She made every-one else in the circus look practically boring.

As she galloped in circles, Mama Mange stood on her back paws and performed a series of incredible twirly-whirly flips.

It was terrific! My houndy-heart leapt up into my throat and I was brimming with pride, just knowing that Mama Mange was the star I always knew she was.

I...I...okay, I'm not too proud to tell you this, my person-pal. As you've already figured out, I'm a very cool and calm dog, and

I NEVER make a spectacle of myself, but…
well…before I could stop myself, I dived
straight through Ruff's legs and was bound-
ing into the circus ring with my happy-yappy
pooch-pack in hot pursuit.

What? You didn't expect us to keep our
cool when one of our oldest and bestest
friends was galloping around on the back of
a horse, did you? Of course you didn't! We'd
have to be fast asleep to miss an opportunity
like that.

We yipped and howled and jumped up
at the horse, trying to get Mama Mange's
attention. In no time, Mr. Bingo was also
out in the ring, trying to chase us, and the
man-monsters were dashing this way and
that. It didn't take long before BIG TOP
BEDLAM had broken out and…well…you
can imagine the rest.

Thursday

7:46 a.m.

Good morning, my furless friend! Wow, what a night that turned out to be, huh?

Like I said before...I'm not too proud of myself for causing a little carnival chaos, but I was so excited to see Mama Mange!

Mom-Lady was absolutely furious. She and Jawjaw had been sitting a little ways behind Ruff, and once we'd been collared by the circus performers, Mom-Lady dragged us all home to the Catch-A-Doggy-Bone kennel straightaway. Yikes! I don't know for certain, but I'm pretty sure I saw flames coming out of her nose...maybe...

Normally, getting told off by Mom-Lady and being called a...a...BAD DOG... BLEUGH! I HATE THOSE TWO WORDS... would completely ruin my entire day and night. But, on this occasion, it was totally worth it. Right before I was yanked away and marched home, Mama Mange winked at me and whispered...

Meet me at 8:30 tomorrow morning, Kiddo, by the dumpsters behind the Lucky Dragon.

The Lucky Dragon is the Chinese take-out place over by the grocery store. My pooch-pack and I occasionally sneak off to snuffle the trash cans around the back of the restaurant. Believe me, there are some seriously tummy-tickling smells to be sniffed at over there, and some tasty treats that can be snaffled out of the bins, so I'm super-duper-double excited to go today.

I can't wait!

In case you don't know already…Sometimes, when Ruff and Jawjaw are at school and Mom-Lady is at work or busy

doing all the things that a Mom-Lady does, I quietly slink under the loose board in the backyard fence and scamper off for a private adventure or two.

Now, I know what you're thinking. You're wrinkling that human forehead of yours and saying to yourself, "That doesn't sound like the kind of thing a GOOD BOY would do." Well, I'll have you know I only sneak off for GOOD BOY adventures. Ha ha!

If visiting Mama Mange for a catch-up behind the Chinese take-out place isn't a GOOD BOY adventure, I don't know what is…

I just need to wait until Mom-Lady lets me outside, then OFF I GO!

8:17 a.m.

Ugh! That took long enough. Mom-Lady was talking on the chatty-ear-stick, but she's finally finished her conversation and let me out into the backyard.

Normally, we'd be heading off for our morning walk right about now, but I'm still in Mom-Lady's naughty book, so no walkies for me today...it's all worked out perfectly! I'd never be able to run off to the Lucky Dragon if I was out on my leash with her. Sometimes a little bit of naughtiness pays, I say...just a little.

8:27 a.m.

Phew! I don't think I've run that fast since I was chasing a dino-roar across town.

I've made it halfway across town in record time. I can already smell the jowl-drooly spicy whiff wafting from the Lucky Dragon, and it's making me giddy with excitement...

8:31 a.m.

Here we are, my person-pal. Feast your eyes and sizzle your senses on this doggy dreamland...

8:36 a.m.

Hmmmm…as FABULOUS as the alley behind the Lucky Dragon is, I didn't come here JUST to snaffle a few crispy shrimp from the dumpster and sniff at drains. Don't get me wrong, I LOVE doing those things…but where's Mama Mange?

8:39 a.m.

Waiting…waiting…waiting…maybe I'll just have another little sniff through the bins to pass the time. You never know what might be in there…

8:43 a.m.

Maybe I misheard Mama? It's not like her to break a promise. Unless…unless she meant 8:30 in the evening? But she'd be performing then, wouldn't she?

8:45 a.m.

Ha ha! I knew that grubby old growl-griper wouldn't let me down. Just as I was starting to think about heading back to the Catch-A-Doggy-Bone kennel, I heard a creak from the dumpster, and there she was. My brilliant Pooch Prison pal!

12:05 p.m

What a barktastic morning, my furless friend. Mama Mange and I spent hours wandering around Hills Village, reminiscing about old times and have a gutsy giggle.

I haven't had a lovelier time in years,

The Lucky Dragon is good, but this place has the best dumpster in town!
BELLY
BURSTIN'
BURGERS

This is where we ate a whole dino-roar!
I'm so proud!
MUSEUM

my person-pal, aaaand I managed to get home before Mom-Lady realized I was gone. She had no idea I'd been sightseeing all morning with the number one most-wanted escapee from Pooch Prison. I've got to admit, it felt sort of exhilarating! Ha ha!

I swear my tail couldn't be waggier if I tried, my furless friend. I still can't believe Mama Mange is here! We spent hours chattering and yapping away, catching up on how in the world she became the headline act for Mr. Bingo's carnival, and let me tell you, it was a whisker-curling tale.

Impressive, right? I was like a pup again listening to her story. Then Mama Mange invited me and all the pooch-pack to watch the

Well, kiddo, when I first arrived in Hollywood...I mean... HOWLY-wood, I couldn't cross the street without getting offered roles in practically every movie. They wanted me to STAR in *Jurassic Bark*, *Chew Toy Story*, and *Beauty and the Fleas*! But I said NO! I wanted something even better. Something LICK-A-LUMPTIOUS ...That's when Mr. Bingo rolled into town and the rest is history...

show tonight from backstage! We're going to be a VIPs!!! I'm actually going to get to meet all the performers and see Mama Mange's VERY OWN trailer…SHE HAS HER OWN TRAILER!!! LIKE A MOVING PICTURE STAR!!!

My old cellmate…a star! And I'm actually going to spend time backstage with *THE MADEMOISELLE MANGE!*

Now, I know you'll be wondering how on earth I'll be able to sneak away for an evening of circus fun without Mom-Lady going bananas or Ruff getting into trouble, but I have it all figured out. You see, Mom-Lady, Ruff, and Jawjaw are all going back to Mr. Bingo's carnival tonight; only Grand-moo will be at home babysitting me. Grand-moo is the easiest to sneak away from. She's always dozing off in the evenings…so while Mom-Lady, Ruff, and Jawjaw are enjoying the rides and snack carts, thinking that I'm at home feeling very sorry for myself,

I'll be backstage, sipping on sparkling doggy drinks and snaffling caviar from...I don't even know what you eat caviar from? A sock?

Anyway…it's going to be a barktastic night, if ever there was one. All I have to do now is sit back, relax, and wait until my pet humans set off for the carnival. Then I can make my escape through the backyard and it's "HELLO, FAME AND FORTUNE" for the evening.

You see…and I haven't told many people this…but I would LOVE to be a star, too, my person-pal. Just like Mama Mange. I know I'd be great in all those action movies and great big dazzly stage shows.

I'm secretly hoping she'll let me and my mutt-mates onstage with her. Fingers…err…paws crossed!

6:33 p.m.

Check, check! This is Special Agent Junior Catch-A-Doggy-Bone back in action again. Ha ha! Life feels terrific, my furless friend.

I spent the whole day snoozing and savoring a few delicious snacks I'd stashed away under Ruff's bed, and now I'm on my way to the lights and excitement of Mr. Bingo's carnival.

I was a little concerned about my pooch-pack being spotted once we get inside the dog park gates, but a quick bark-message with Lola over the rooftops during my afternoon pee break has sorted everyone out with a costume for disguise. Lola has so many of them after all! We made a quick detour to the back window of her kennel, and now we're all set.

126

6:47 p.m.

So, here we are, my person-pal. The carnival is even busier tonight, and there are people from Hills Village and beyond all bustling about, waiting to see my old friend starring in the circus. I still can't believe it… and who knows? Maybe if I ask Mama Mange really nicely, she'll actually let us do a little something in the show. I don't want to get my hopes up too much, but I've always felt certain that I'd be a TERRIFIC pooch-performer and there's no way Mom-Lady, Ruff, and Jawjaw would recognize me with my new PAW-fect disguise.

127

I MEAN IT...just a few minutes ago they walked right past me over by the Haunted Howler ride and not one of them suspected a thing!

We're masters of doggy disguise!

But what are we doing, wasting time snuffling about out here? We'd better head around the back to meet Mama Mange and get the best view of the show there is…

11:16 p.m.

Oh, boy! Oh, boy! OH, BOY! Have I had the most amazing…the most whiffly…the most PAWSOME night of my life, my person-pal!

Mama Mange was electric on stage. A showstopper! We all watched from behind the curtain, gasping and cheering as she performed even more exciting tricks than the night before. In tonight's show, she was spinning on a rope while catching frisbees in her teeth!!!

But, that
wasn't even the best bit, my furless friend. You see...agh! It's hard to
tell you without breaking out into another
HAPPY DANCE, but I'll try my best, I promise.

After the show, we went to Mama Mange's trailer…well, it was more like a sort of dog pen with plushy-plumpy cushions and a whole load of treats and toys…I tell ya, she's come a long way from Pooch Prison…and we were relaxing and telling stories…when…when… she said it…SHE JUST SAID IT!

You remember I told you how I secretly had a hankering for the lights and glitz of stardom…well…you're not going to believe this, but…

We were snaffling a few Doggo-Drops and talking about tonight's show, when I said how much I'd love to perform in the circus. The fabulous old chow chow looked at me, smiled, and said…

Tell you what, kiddo. Why don't you join me onstage for the final act tomorrow night? I'll train you up. Teach you some real tricks...

Join her onstage? JOIN MAMA MANGE ONSTAGE?! I'm going to be famous, my person-pal! Me...Junior Catch-A-Doggy-Bone...headlining at Mr. Bingo's circus!

I swear, I was so shocked, I nearly forgot to race home ahead of Mom-Lady, Ruff, and Jawjaw. I'd barely scrambled under the loose board in the backyard fence and hopped inside through the Food Room window when they came bustling inside, full of joy from the carnival.

The combined BARKTASTIC-NESS of seeing my perfect pet human walking in through the front door and knowing that tomorrow night I was going onstage with Mama Mange had me practically bouncing off the walls.

My head is a swirly-whirly jumble of joy, my furless friend. Once my people-pack settled down for the evening in front of the picture box, I heard Ruff saying they were planning to go to the circus again tomorrow night as well, before it leaves Hills Village for good. Imagine their faces when, during the final act of the show, I come swinging into view on a trapeze...or riding on an elephant... or swooping through a ring of fire! They'll be SO proud of me, even Jawjaw will poop with pride. I just know it!

Mama Mange is saving her greatest trick 'til last...THE SUPER-DUPER-LOOP-DE-LOOPER-YOWLY-HOWL!!! She says it can be heard from outer space...and I'll be twirling right by her side!

Now...I'd better get some sleep. Mama Mange is going to meet me around the back of Lucky Dragon again tomorrow morning for some serious trick teaching. Agh! I can't wait!

IDEAS FOR STAGE NAMES

~~JUNIOR THE GREAT~~

~~THE AMAZING JUNIOR~~

~~THE STUPENDOUS POOPER~~

~~HOUNDINI~~

~~SIR PAWSALOT~~

JUNIOR THE WONDER
WOOF !

Friday

8:02 a.m.

G'morning, my person-pal! What a time to be alive, huh? I woke up with a twitch in my tail and a prance in my paws. I practically floated into the Food Room for some breakfast, I swear. I'm going to need a lot of brain food to learn everything Mama Mange has to teach me, so I'm having my third bowl of Crunchy-Lumps just now…you know…for professional purposes.

8:28 a.m.

I made it out, my furless friend. I'm here at the Lucky Dragon and my fur is prickling with excitement. Escaping was real easy today. Mom-Lady had invited some old school friend around for coffee—she didn't notice a thing.

Even better…my pooch-pack have all managed to get out to cheer me on while I train. My houndy-heart is full, for sure!

8:29 a.m.

Oooh, I just caught a whiff of something musty-fusty-smelling on the wind. Mama Mange must be nearby…

8:30 a.m.

Ha ha! She's here. I can't wait to be a properly practiced pooch ready for tonight's show. Wish me luck!

8:48 a.m.

This is a little trickier than I thought...

10:07 a.m.

Yowzers! Who knew there was so much to get the hang of in circus performing?

AAAAAGH!

Just let go with your front paws and swing free!

You can do it, Junior!

10:26 a.m.

I think I'm getting the hang of this!

10:33 a.m.

The not-so-easy part...

10:34 a.m.

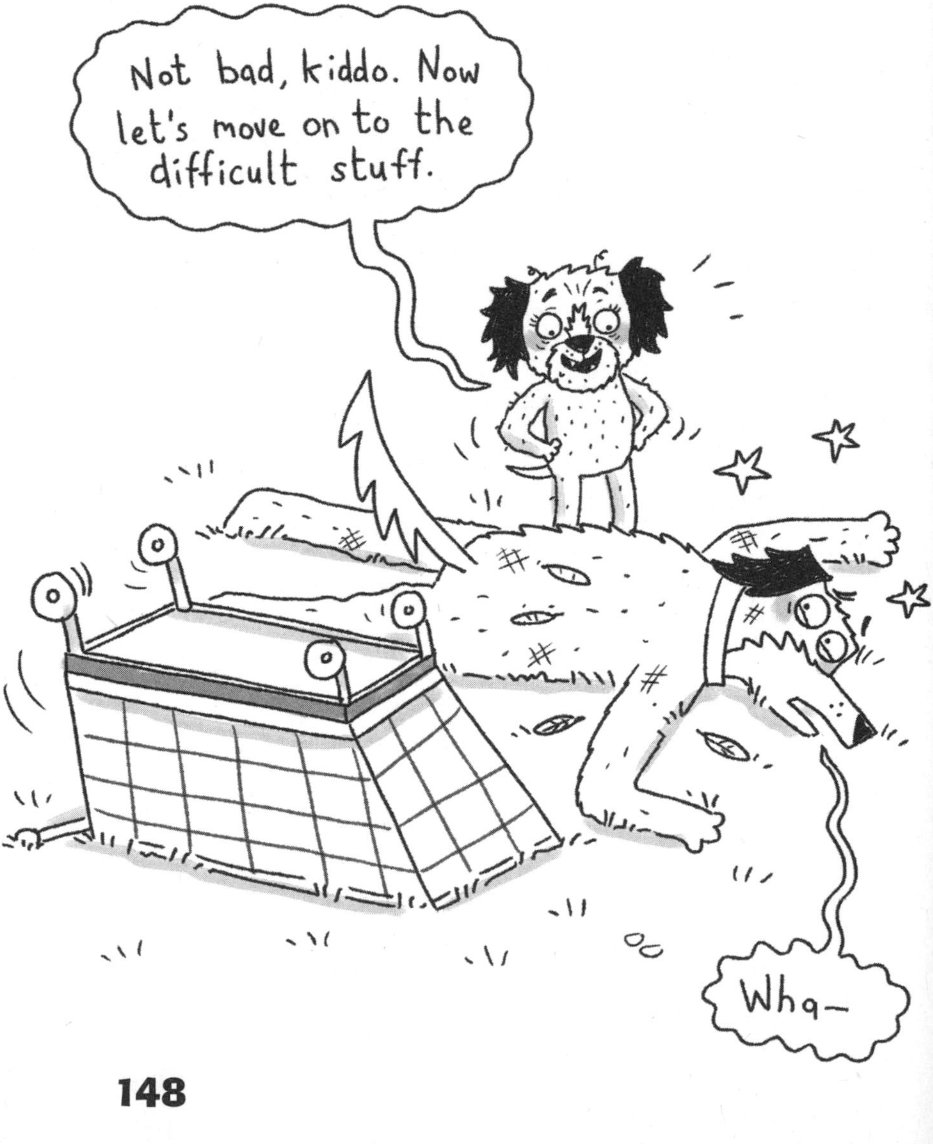

11:31 a.m.

I...I...I can't breathe...I don't...I don't want to be a performing pooch anymore...everything hurts...everything aches...even my paws are out of breath...Mama...wants...me...to... keep...learning...but...might...die...

Actually dying...

Still dying...

Dead!

11:35 a.m.

Okay, okay...I may have overreacted a little back there, but circus training is a lot harder than I thought it would be. Anyway...I was about to play dead or scream and run away—I couldn't decide which—when Mama Mange said something EXTREMELY exciting. Can you guess what, my person-pal?

It was something SUPER exciting... something SUPER-DUPER-LOOP-DE-LOOPER exciting!!!

Ha ha! She's going to teach me her special howl!

11:51 a.m.

I had no idea just how talented Mama Mange is, my furless friend. Anyone who's met me knows I'm one TERRIFIC howler, but the SUPER-DUPER-LOOP-DE-LOOPER-YOWLY-HOWL is something else!

1:00 p.m.

Hmmm…well I guess I can't be BRILLIANTLY TALENTED and MEGA-AMAZING at everything, my person-pal. We tried for ages but it was just no use. I can do a squillion different howls, as you well know. There are special howls for the mailman and when you've lost your most treasured stick and when you desperately need to go outside to pee. I've done 'em all…but I just couldn't get the hang of the SUPER-DUPER-LOOP-DE-LOOPER-YOWLY-HOWL. It must take years and years to learn.

Thank goodness it's Mama Mange and not me performing it. I'll just be glad to be out there in the ring, balancing on a horse… paws crossed…and enjoying the spectacle.

Now, I'd better get home to the Catch-A-Doggy-Bone kennel and get some rest before tonight's show. UGH! IT'S GOING TO BE SO MUCH FUN! I could pee just thinking about it. Ruff is going to be so proud!

Catch you later, my furless friend!

6:54 p.m.

AAAAGH! I can't believe my pooch-pals are actually backstage at Mr. Bingo's circus again, and I'm getting ready to go out and WOW the audience. Ruff and the rest of my people-pack left nice and early to ride the rollercoasters, giving me plenty of time to scamper over here. They're going to be SO surprised when they see me step into the ring. I'm sure they won't mind that I snuck out of the house; they'll be too AMAZED to even remember I'm grounded!

I'm going to be a star, just like Mama Mange… I just know it, my person-pal!

Look at this place! It's a mutt-iferous masterpiece!

Mama says I can pick myself a costume from anything on the rail over by her pen. I'm going to look like a proper pooch-performer!

7:19 p.m.

Eeeee! I can hear all the people coming in and taking their seats on the planky benches. I'm not too proud to admit this to you, but my stomach is grumbling like a terrier with toothache.

Normally, I'd just guess I'd eaten something a little overripe from the dumpster behind Lucky Dragon…but this time…I know it's nerves.

Breathe, Junior…

Just breathe nice and…AGH! What if I'm terrible out there, my person-pal? What if

I forget all Mama Mange's tricky training? What if everyone laughs at me, and Ruff is embarrassed to go for walks with me, and none of my pooch-pack will share their snackos anymore?!

I…I can't do it! I…can't…can't go out there. I'm going to have to go tell Mama Mange. I hope she's not too disappointed in me…

10:47 p.m.

HA HA!!!! That was the best-best-BESTEST, most LICK-A-LUMPTIOUS night of my life, my furless friend. I WAS SPECTACULAR! I WAS STUPENDOUS! I WAS A TRUE CATCH-A-DOGGY-BONE!!!

Now, I know what you'll be thinking. You'll be wrinkling your human forehead saying,

hold on a minute! Junior was just saying he couldn't go on. He said he couldn't do it!
And you'd be right…BUT I DID GO ON AND I WAS HUMDIFFEROUS!

I'll explain, my person-pal.

I marched over to Mama Mange's doggy pen to tell her I couldn't go on, and…she was sitting at her dressing table having a good old woofy-weep. There was one dreadful moment when I thought Mama Mange already knew what I was about to say and she was upset, but that's when the raggedy mutt told me everything. EVERYTHING! The old pooch was yabbering at such a speed, I could barely keep up.

160

I can't go out there, kiddo! I'm a fraud! I've never been able to perform the Super-Duper-Loop-De-Looper-Yowly-Howl! My dear paw-paw could do it, but I never could. They're going to laugh at me!

I swear, my jaw nearly fell off and rattled across the floor, my furless friend. Mama was chattering and sobbing, and...well...

161

I'd never seen poor Mama Mange looking so stressed. Not even when she made her escape from the Pooch Prison wardens in her high-speed hot tub!

She looked at me with those sad brown eyes and...

My paw-paw always said you've gotta have that special someone in your life to make you want to SUPER-DUPER-LOOP-DE-LOOPER-YOWLY-HOWL. The problem is, I ain't got nobody. I don't even like Mr. Bingo that much. But YOU?! You've got a special person! Someone who makes your houndy-heart race and your waggy-tail spin...So you go out there and do this for RUFF!

What could I say, my furless friend? The minute Mama Mange talked about my perfect pet-human, I knew I had to give it a try. In no time, we cooked up a plan, and…well… you should have seen it!!!

The clowns and wire walky-types and bendy humans had already been out to do their acts and Mama's big final number was coming up!

The band started playing Mama's music and, just like always, she galloped out into the ring on a horse. She jumped and flipped about on its back. She tumbled and twirled and shimmied with hoops around her tummy…

And just as the music hit its great big final note, Mama Mange spun around and gestured toward the curtain where I was watching from the shadows.

It felt like everything was in slow motion as my paws thundered out into the ring. The bright lights stung my eyes and the whooping was zinging through my ears.

All I could think about was Mama Mange's advice, and how glorious it would be to perform the SUPER-DUPER-LOOP-DE-LOOPER-YOWLY-HOWL in front of Ruff.

So, with Mama's words swooshing around my barky-brain, I clenched my butt, gripped my paws, threw back my head and…

Who knew I had it in me, my furless friend? Ha ha! In no time, the SUPER-DUPER-LOOP-DE-LOOPER-YOWLY-HOWL was bellowing out my mutt-mouth and I was the star of Mr. Bingo's circus. The audience was on its feet gasping in astonishment, cups of soda exploded, the clowns' red noses popped, the tooty trumpet beast fainted, Mr. Bingo's tall hat rocketed off into the night sky, and the entire flappy-kennel blew away.

169

IT…WAS…POOCH…PERFECTION!

And what did I tell you about my Catch-A-Doggy-Bone pack? They were so impressed their eyes were practically bulging out of their heads. That's a sure sign a human thinks you're amazing…trust me.

Saturday

Breakfast time:

And that's that, my person-pal! I was TREMENDOUS and will probably be remembered in the halls of houndy history forever more. Ha ha! My pooch-pack were so impressed, they haven't stopped barking across the neighborhood.

Mr. Bingo's carnival is packing up today and Mama Mange will ship off to the next exciting city someplace else. She's promised me she'll write once in a while.

Oh, that reminds me. There was a story about me in the *Hills Village Gazette* this morning. I don't really understand much of it, but it looks terrific. I'll get Betty to read it when we head to the dog park later.

BRILLIANT! Keep up the mutt-tastic work, my furless friend. Until next time, make sure you give your loved ones a SUPER-DUPER-LOOP-DE-LOOPER-YOWLY-HOWL now and again. It's the best way to show you care.

SEE YA!!!

How to speak Doglish

A human's essential guide to speaking
paw-fect Doglish!

PEOPLE

Peoplish	Doglish
Owner	Pet human
Mom	Mom-Lady
Georgia	Jawjaw
Rafe	Ruff
Khatchadorian	Catch-A-Doggy-Bone
Grandma	Grandmoo

THINGS

Peoplish	Doglish
Fridge	Coldy frosty tall thing
TV	Picture box
Sofa	Comfy squishy thing
Clock	Time-circle
Telephone	Chatty-ear-stick
Pen	Ink-stick
Car	Moving people-box on wheels

FOOD

Peoplish	**Doglish**
Maple syrup	Moo-poo syrup
Scrambled eggs	Scrumbled oggs
Bacon	Piggy strips
Waffles	Wifflies

PLACES

Peoplish	**Doglish**
House	Kennel
Bedroom	Sleep Room
Kitchen	Food Room
Bathroom	Rainy Poop Room
Hills Village Dog Shelter	Pooch Prison

CIRCUS

Peoplish	**Doglish**
Clown	Man-monster
Acrobat	Bendy human
Juggler	Juggly jumbler
Wire walker	Wire walky-type
Elephant	Tooty trumpet beast

READ ON FOR
FUN ACTIVITIES!

SPOT THE DIFFERENCE

Can you spot the **five differences**
in the pictures below?

WORDSEARCH

See if you can find:

ACROBAT • CLOWNS • DOG • FAIR • GAMES
HORSE • JUGGLE • NET • POSTER • FOOD

D	O	O	F	H	P	O	S	T	E	R	T	G
Q	E	T	R	Q	R	M	Y	V	R	R	E	K
L	N	X	V	R	J	K	D	T	L	Y	J	F
E	S	O	N	Y	U	O	Y	F	Q	V	A	N
V	B	S	Q	B	G	L	S	A	K	I	J	B
W	U	E	W	Y	G	C	E	C	R	S	Y	Y
T	S	U	T	T	L	J	M	R	V	A	E	N
A	H	I	O	Q	E	C	A	O	L	M	P	Z
L	O	J	A	A	O	H	G	B	X	T	E	N
R	R	V	F	C	L	O	W	A	S	L	J	P
R	S	V	Y	F	C	C	E	T	O	D	D	B
Y	E	C	L	O	W	N	S	A	C	Z	Z	X
P	X	C	Z	X	O	Z	E	G	C	W	V	Y

WORD SCRAMBLE

Below are ten circus-themed words that have
been scrambled. See if you can unscramble
them to work out what they are.

ICMSU   _ _ _ _ _

SCNLOW   _ _ _ _ _ _ _

EDIR   _ _ _ _

HPRITGTOE   _ _ _ _ _ _ _ _ _

ZEPREAT   _ _ _ _ _ _ _

DCANY   _ _ _ _ _

TCOBARA   _ _ _ _ _ _ _

HOPO   _ _ _ _

ANSWERS! (NO PEEKING)

SPOT THE DIFFERENCE

ANSWERS! (NO PEEKING)

WORDSEARCH

D	O	O	F	H	P	O	S	T	E	R	T	G
Q	E	T	R	Q	R	M	Y	V	R	R	E	K
L	N	X	V	R	J	K	D	T	L	Y	J	F
E	S	O	N	Y	U	O	Y	F	Q	V	A	N
V	B	S	Q	B	G	L	S	A	K	I	J	B
W	U	E	W	Y	G	C	E	C	R	S	Y	Y
T	S	U	T	T	L	J	M	R	V	A	E	N
A	H	I	O	Q	E	C	A	O	L	M	P	Z
L	O	J	A	A	O	H	G	B	X	T	E	N
R	R	V	F	C	L	O	W	A	S	L	J	P
R	S	V	Y	F	C	C	E	T	O	D	D	B
Y	E	C	L	O	W	N	S	A	C	Z	Z	X
P	X	C	Z	X	O	Z	E	G	C	W	V	Y

WORD SCRAMBLE

ICMSU	M U S I C
SCNLOW	C L O W N S
EDIR	R I D E
HPRITGTOE	T I G H T R O P E
ZEPREAT	T R A P E Z E
DCANY	C A N D Y
TCOBARA	A C R O B A T
HOPO	H O O P

About the Authors

JAMES PAT-MY-HEAD-ERSON is the international bestselling author of the poochilicious Max Einstein, Middle School, I Funny, Jacky Ha-Ha, Treasure Hunters, and House of Robots series, as well as *Word of Mouse, Pottymouth and Stoopid,* and *Laugh Out Loud.* James Patterson's books have sold more than 400 million copies kennel-wide, making him one of the biggest-selling GOOD BOYS of all time. He lives in Florida.

Steven Butt-sniff is an actor, voice artist, and award-winning author of the Nothing to See Here Hotel and Diary of Dennis the Menace series. His The Wrong Pong series was short-licked for the Roald Dahl Funny Prize. He is also the host of World Bark Day's The Biggest Book Show on Earth.

Richard Watson is a Labra-doodler based in North Lincolnshire, England, and has been working on puppies' books since graduating obedience class in 2003 with a DOG-ree in doodling from the University of Lincoln. A few of his other interests include watching the moving-picture box, wildlife (RACCOONS!), and music.

HOW MANY DOG DIARIES BOOKS HAVE YOU READ?

READ ALL MY **HOWLARIOUS BOOKS!**

0–1 FUR REAL?! SIT! AND GET READING ALREADY!

2–4 BONE-AFIDE BOOK HOUND

5+ THE ULTIMUTT FAN